William Channing Gannett

A year of miracle

A poem in four sermons

William Channing Gannett

A year of miracle
A poem in four sermons

ISBN/EAN: 9783337266134

Printed in Europe, USA, Canada, Australia, Japan

Cover: Foto ©Andreas Hilbeck / pixelio.de

More available books at **www.hansebooks.com**

A YEAR OF MIRACLE.

A POEM IN FOUR SERMONS.

BY

W. C. GANNETT.

———•———

BOSTON:
GEO. H. ELLIS, 141 FRANKLIN STREET.
1882.

IN, TO, FOR

UNITY CHURCH,

St. Paul.

CONTENTS.

TREASURES OF THE SNOW.

I.

TREASURES OF THE SNOW.

IF a sunset were as rare as a comet, the people would all be out upon the hill-tops — astronomers with their telescopes, poets with their pens, artists with their brushes — to capture what they could of it, and give it immortality. Or, if only once in a year the eastern skies held sunrise, we should be out of bed betimes that morning to watch the gold and crimson pageant passing up the sky. But because these glories face us every day, we are color-blind to them. Still worse with glories that are near as well as frequent. We envy a friend starting for Europe, going where there is " so much to see," we say,— Alps, cathedrals, and old art: as if a year spent in the nearest pasture would not crowd our mind with miracles, if only we had eyes to see with!

" Hast thou entered into the treasures of the snow?" Probably not: for he who asked the

question spoke of a treasure-chamber, rare in
Bible lands, but opened to us anew with each
December; open all the winter long; opened
in every door-yard and at every window-pane:
and a palace so common and so near as that is
not a palace to eyes that chiefly love the far
things and the rare. But, if only once in many
years those wondrous treasure-chambers were
unlocked, how we should hand down the tradi-
tion,—like men who, having caught one glimpse
of some new Mexico, should prattle of an El
Dorado all their lives! At Beaufort in South
Carolina, the whole population, black and white,
turned out one winter's day to see — a frozen
pond! A northern teacher, dying on one of
the Sea Islands there in slavery-time, was en-
shrined in the memory of her southern friends
by a snow-fall, that happened to float down on
the north wind just after the stranger had been
laid in her fresh grave: it seemed like a flight
of friendly angels from her home-land, because,
like angels' visits, its comings were so few and
far between. The Siamese prince heard of
"solid water" with complete unfaith,—a miracle too great for even Oriental credence. And
in Abyssinia, far under the tropic sky, Bruce,

the hunter for the sources of the Nile, came to a village where

"An old man told him, with a grave surprise
   Which made his childlike wonder almost grand
How, in his youth, there fell from out the skies
   A feathery whiteness over all the land,—
A strange, soft, spotless something, pure as light,
   For which their questioned language had no name,—
That shone and sparkled for a day and night,
   Then vanished all as weirdly as it came ;
Leaving no vestige, gleam, or hue or scent
   On the round hill or in the purple air,
To certify their mute bewilderment
   That such a presence had indeed been there ! "

And they had named their village from that one unprecedented snow-fall. Thus, men stand in awe before the snow where its treasures are rare.

In the Hebrew land it was by no means so unheard of. It glistens on the top of Hermon, and lies deep in the high ravines of Lebanon, until the summer is far advanced ; and, unless the climate be changed, Jesus, when a boy, had chances to make snow-balls now and then on the hill-tops around Nazareth. Yet, in that grand drama of Job in which God asks the man our question, "Hast thou entered into the treasures of the snow?" it is ranked among the major wonders,— with the morning stars and the sea, with the lightnings and Leviathan and death. Majestic grouping, is it not? But, after all, the morning-stars and the lightnings and death belong to the every-days; and the writer mentions also the dew and the rain and the wild goats, and the young ravens hungry in the winter,— things small and common enough. Perhaps in his case it was not so much the rareness that made the appreciation, but that he had poet's eyes to see with. The poet is the man with double vision, one who is at once near-sighted and far-sighted, who sees the closer things as wonders because he sees their far relations too. Where we say "poet," we might say simply "seer." At all events, this Bible-poet, phrasing a question for God's lips, phrases it fitly for the God of Nature to ask. I hear it uttered thus: "Thou *seest* the pebble, the rain-drop, the grass-blade, the dust-mote, the snow-flake: hast thou *entered into their treasures?* I make my worlds out of them!"

To-day, again, the question lies written on the ground in our fresh snow-fall. We will accept its invitation, and try to enter in a little way.

The colors of the spring dawn slowly, the color of the winter in an hour,— when all is ready. Not until all is ready. A night, away back in October, sets a frosty seal upon the grass and trees; and Nature knows the sign and begins to unrobe her for the sleep. Her colors, dropping back from green through yellow, orange, and the reds, fade at last to browns and russets; and then she rustles into nakedness. Just when she is lying down, the Indian season comes, and with a gentle dream of summer she drowses into death. The birds have flown; the flowers, too. The ferns and vines, the little children of the woodlands, have vanished to their secret nurseries underground. The hills grow bleak and bare; the fields roughen into ridge and furrow; and broken stalks, and the stones, hidden since the May-days, stand stiffly out again in sight. The trees now stand forlorn with empty nests,—" bare, ruined choirs, where late the sweet birds sang." Their tossing arms lash the ground with wild, black shadows through the windy, moonlit nights. The cold increases; the winds search and whistle and sting; the pools skim over of a morning; the cattle huddle in the field; the fowls stand drearily in the lee of the bush; faces redden on the street; and, under the stars, fire-light gleams through the window-panes.

Meanwhile, the home-life deepens. As a friend once said to me, the seasons indoors seem to just reverse the order of the outward seasons. As the leaves are fading in the fall, we feel within our bodies and our minds a bracing *spring;* plans gather vigor, and we bend ourselves for the hard work of the year. The winter brings heart and mind to their full force of growth. Nature's winter is the human summer-time. Then, spring begins to make us languid. And the busy summer of earth-life brings to ourselves a pause and rest and comparative inaction, like an inward winter. Reckoning this way by the spirit's calendar, Thanksgiving Day is Easter; and the Easter is Thanksgiving Day for a winter's inward harvests; for then we shall have gathered in and barned away in memory what we have read and thought and done in our growing hours, while the snow lay outside on the ground.

So, as Nature is getting ready for what may happen out of doors, indoors it is all astir. Hands oftener meet other hands in works of service, and hearts are closer drawn to hearts. The books come forth in the long evenings, the story-telling begins, the fathers and mothers gather the children around their knees by the cheerful blaze,—that blaze itself the sunshine of old springs and summers in the far-off past. Over all within, without, is God, who careth for us thus; who made those summers of old and stored their heat, who is preparing now the seasons of our immortality. At last, all is ready.

As we sit and work, or sit and dream, a day comes in which a stillness falls. A hush is on the earth; a gray sky is overspread above; an uneasiness is in the air which is not wind. Go to the window and watch. A few heralds clad in white come floating down, turning this way, turning that way, like scouts seeking for paths and camping-places. Then, of a sudden, the thick, dull sky is alive with trooping forms! The ways of the air are filled with the army of the Snow! Their tread is not with sound, but second by second they arrive, and alight, and possess themselves of the hills and the hollows. The fields grow silent and white with their gleaming camp. Whole States are changed in a few hushed moments; and no stone, no twig, no cranny, is forgotten. Only the all-enclosing air could do it; and the air has done it! The signs of human parting and property are blotted out in indiscriminate conquest as Nature seizes again on her old patrimony of the earth, ignoring man who has marked out his farms upon it. All the men of the land in armies could not work such uniform obliteration in a year. All the men of the land, as builders, could not fashion in a century such rare and universal architecture as the hurrying wind and snow build up together on tree and house and rock and fence and everything that offers niche or pedestal.

How they come trooping down! Hour after hour we watch, and still the host comes marching in,— now in steady, downright phalanxes,— now swerving, whole solid columns, in rapid flanking movements, — now in little whirling charges dashing in from this side and from that in furious mêlée.

And each of the mighty army is clad in crystal panoply. Let us waylay some of the stragglers, and examine them. That crystal panoply is our first "treasure." The captives are by no means clad alike, however. Upwards of a thousand differing forms of snow-flakes have been observed. I have seen a book containing some two hundred of them figured. Here are simple prisms, three-sided or six-sided. Here are some tiny pyramids one-thirtieth of an inch in height, yet as mathematically perfect in their lines as the Great Pyramid of Egypt in its best estate. And here are prisms capped with the pyramids. More familiar to us are these star-like forms; but verily, as with the stars above, one differeth from another in its glory. The simplest is this wherein six prisms radiate from a centre, like wheel-spokes from a hub. Then, on both spokes and hub Nature sets to work to play her variations. Each ray, beset on either side with tinier prisms, takes on the semblance of a fern-leaf; and the species seem to vary in outline as the fern-species vary in the summer woods. That centre, which I ignobly called the "hub," enlarges to a six-sided plate, or often is itself a star whose glittering arms stem off to be tipped with little trefoils or rosettes. Here lies a star within a star, and that within another star, and all within a fourth! Some of these centres are wrought in finest open-work, others are filled white to the rim; but under the

microscope we could see these last all fretted
over with fairy hieroglyphics, silvery mosaics
marked off in triangles and hexagons. In one
variety the crossing prisms make you think
of the child's puzzle, where the little wooden
blocks lock together into a tight nest. Another form seems different from all the rest:
it is a star set at each end of a prism like the
two wheels on an axle-tree. Up in the Polar
seas, Dr. Scoresby one day found his ship's
deck covered three inches deep with such little
air-chariots.

But these dainty forms, and this variety in
their daintiness, are not the only treasures of
the snow-flake. Through all that variety runs
identity. The flakes are akin in their deeper
being, as negro and Esquimaux, cannibal and
Quaker, are yet all one in human nature. Snow-
nature is bound by a law of sixes. The sides of
every prism and pyramid meet at one angle,—
that of 60°,— or its multiples: the rays of every
star diverge at that one angle; every vein upon
those little fern-leaves joins its stem at that one
angle, or its multiples. The stars are all six-
rayed, or rarely twelve; the centres all hexag-
onal. Watch the flakes of a whole winter's

storms, climb Chimborazo, go to the Pole, or make your mimic snow-storm for yourself inside a chemist's bottle,—never will you find a finished star with five rays or with seven, or with that law of the angles broken. The rays themselves are broken, but never that creative law. Bruised, shattered, huddled together, the snow-flakes reach us ; but through all bruise and shatter that law of " sixes " lies plain upon them. By that they are born and live and die.

Is it not very impressive and awe-ful,—these mathematics carried down to the microscopic measurements, these " ethics of the dust," as Ruskin calls them,— the grand legislation of the universe laid thus upon its invisible atoms!

Now, who can explain such wondrous birth and fashioning? Shall we answer for the snow-flake what George MacDonald makes the baby answer for itself ?—

" Where did you come from, baby dear ?
Out of the everywhere into here !

" How did it all just come to be you ?
God thought about me,— and so I grew !

" Where did you get that pearly ear?
God spoke, and it came out to hear ! "

Did God look, and the snow-flake come out to be looked at ? Somewhat so would the old Genesis and Psalm-writers of the eastern land have solved the problem. The answer then was simple,—"He saith to the snow, Be thou upon the 'earth." Somewhat thus would the poets and the religious feeling of every land and time solve it, our own as much as all the rest. Did we wish to be a little more knowing, we might answer, "The air was full of va- por, and the thermometer fell to 32°, and so, of course, it snowed." Of course, it did; but did you ever think of it ? — "of course" is our appeal to the unsolved mystery, the Course of Nature.

The scientific men, however, who go dredging in those deeps of mystery bring up, at least, a guess. They tell us that all substances (solid granite and hard iron as well as lightest gas) consist of atoms suspended in an ether, an ether that is ever thrilling with invisible vibrations of heat and light and electricity. To their eyes, the universe, through and through, is in unceas- ing motion. And when we say, "the thermom- eter falls," what we mean, in brief, is this : the water-atoms, while the water is in the form of vapor, move loosely, freely, distantly; but, as the cold increases, this heat-dance slackens, and the atoms gradually close together, until the vapor, changing form, becomes a "liquid"; with still greater cold, the atoms keep on approaching one another, until by a second transformation they are — not fast-locked, by any means — but faster-locked, into what we call the "solid" form,— and thus the snow is born!

And it is by a measured march that the vapor-atoms have thus closed and coalesced. Each Lilliputian knows his place, and like a veteran soldier moves in rhythms to his post within the flake. In rhythms: the Egyptian sculptures show us pictures of the way in which the great stones of their pyramids were dragged, in that day before the engines had appeared. Five hundred men are seen tugging at the ropes and rollers; but, to secure the pull together which alone would move the block, there stands among them a musician playing on an instrument. And the stones are thus drawn by music to their courses in the pyramid. Now fancy the water-vapor atoms marching in,— through the billionth of an inch, invisible hosts to inaudible music,— to build up the snow-flake! What time they keep!

But whence comes that variety in building-plans,— now star, now prism, and now pyramid? Doubtless from some difference in temperature, or in the amount of vapor in the air, or in the rush-rate of the storm.   In still days, with the temperature not far below the freezing-point, the stars fall large and fair.   The stars that fall from Minnesota skies are, on the average, much more perfect than those that light upon the sea-coasts. Dr. Kane describes the snow that wraps the scanty vegetation near the Pole as a three-layered blanket: first, a light and air-filled layer in the early winter; then, the solid, tight-packed crystals of mid-winter; then, another porous stratum in the spring.   We will not say, with one who called our admiration to the snow-flake a hundred years ago, that "the more *common* forms are due to temperature, etc., but for the infinite variety of types we must go to the will and pleasure of the Great First Cause."   For the flower rare here lives somewhere as the weed, the exception here is somewhere the rule; and the weed, the rule, the every-day miracle remains *the* miracle.   The *next* snow-flake will. startle us, if we can only see it as it is.

How big or, rather, how little are those atoms,

is our natural wonder, as we hear such state-
ments made. They have never yet been seen;
they are merely guessed at to explain certain
phenomena that are seen; so that their size,
or want of size, is rather problematical. But
the calculators have tried their best. After different methods of approximation, Sir William
Thomson, the great English mathematician an-
nounced his provisional answer thus: If a drop
of water should be magnified to the size of
the earth,— one drop swollen to the planet's
size,— then the constituent molecules of that
drop would probably be larger than shot, and
probably smaller than cricket-balls! When you
have taken this in thoroughly, then remember
that each molecule of water is itself compounded
of atoms more minute of oxygen and hydrogen.
Did I not rightly say "hosts," to hint the census
of the snow-flake? To watch a dew-drop gather
on a grass-blade, and whiten into frost, is as if
one standing on a mountain-top were watching
the muster of a mighty army in the dim lands
far below.

Even if this atomic theory were known to be
certain fact, instead of being merely to-day's
wisest guess, have we *explained* the snow-flake

yet? Hardly more than by our bare thermometer statement. We have only moved our "of course" a little farther back, where still the mystery remains. What, and whence, are the atoms? How came each to know its place and be able to move in rhythms to it? And by what force impelled!

Remember that no particle of moisture is debarred this transfiguration. The broad ocean and the land-locked pond and the roadside pool may all be one in destiny, because one in their origin. No ditch so grimy with reeking poison but its vapor, mounting, may take on the form of stars and become a pure and white-winged wonder of the air. However poor its earth-lot, this heaven awaits it. Could we question every flake that wanders to our window-ledge about its past, we should hear a mingled song like that the Christians fancy of the hosts before the throne of God :—

> I came from off mid-ocean,
>   I in a wild-flower lay,
> I came from a brook on a mountain-side,
>   And I from Niagara's spray;
> And I was a tear in a mother's eyes
>   For a little one gone away.

What histories they could tell, what gospels of beauty preach, these little stars, if they could "sing together" to our hearing! And all share in the glory and the song, whether destined for the slow-dying glacier, or born to flutter for an instant, light upon the stream, and vanish.

We have entered only one of the treasure-chambers. We will not go through all. The Pope's palace, the Vatican, has over four thousand rooms. I know not how many we might expect to find in this tiny house not made with hands.

But let us linger a moment to think of the *physical power* involved in an inch-deep snow-storm. The amount of heat absorbed and liberated would work the engines of the world. First, think what masses of water have to be raised as vapor from the ocean-top, and drifted far and wide across the lands, to prepare that even gray sky which made us say, " It is going to snow,"— and try to conceive or calculate the heat absorbed in that operation. Then think of the snow that covers all the State an inch deep in an hour, and try to conceive or calculate the amount of heat liberated in this reverse operation as the vapor falls back not only to the liquid, but the solid state.   Let me state it thus, calculating from some of Tyndall's figures: A boy grasps a handful from the fence-top and pats it to a ball, weighing half a pound,— intending it for his friend a few yards off.   But the force employed to make from water-vapor that snow of which he made his ball, would fling a ball weighing one hundred pounds two-thirds of a mile into the air.   The force employed to make the half-pound of water-vapor out of the original oxygen and hydrogen would fling a hundred-pound ball nearly five miles into the air!   *That* force summoned to make one half-pound of snow!   Then think of the engines at work to make the whole snow-storm!   Think of the might, as well as tenderness, it took to press those few frost-flowers upon your window-panes! You did not dream what strong hands lurked in your bed-chamber through the winter night.

The *color* of the snow is another of its treasures.   To enter into that, we must open the door of the rainbow chamber, where we should see, besides the snow, such things as the white clouds and the ocean spray and the crests of breaking waves, and learn how in all of them the ravelled prism-colors are woven into white again.   It is the mingling of the infinitely many reflections that flash from the sides and angles of the tiny prisms and pyramids and stars that make the dazzling whiteness. Crush the transparent ice, and its grains will whiten also, for the same reason.

And we will crush it, for we ought not to pass by the wondrous structure of the ice without a word of awe. Ice is simply a solid firmament, so to speak, of snow-stars; a fossil forest, as it were, of the snow-fern leaves, of that silvery foliage with which by winter moonlight every window grows to a leafy bower of air-plants. Ask Tyndall to send a beam of sunlight through a block of ice, and place a lens in front, so as to catch a magnified image of what happens on his screen. As in the night-heavens, when a wind sweeps the clouds away, suddenly the stars appear, so here within the ice-slab first one star, then another, looks out at us; then the constellations thicken; and, as the process goes on, the rays begin to change to petals, and presently the screen is covered with the fern-leaves. As if some night, while we watched those old constellations in the sky, they should begin to arrange themselves in blossom-forms before our eyes. It is only melting ice. What has happened? Let Tyndall himself tell: "Silently and symmetrically the crystallizing force built the atoms up, silently and symmetrically the sunbeam has taken them down. What beauty latent in a block of common ice! And only think of lavish Nature operating thus throughout the world. Every atom of the solid ice which sheets the frozen lakes of the north has been fixed according to this law. Nature 'lays her beams in music,' and it is the function of science to purify our organs, so as to enable us to hear the strain."

Will you step once more to the window, and watch the snow come down? How the flakes drift and whirl and dart and light and whirl again! If ever chance, if ever chaos, then here. And yet we know it must be fact that not one motion of the little Arabs but happens under eternal law; that not one flies or loiters save as the steady forces guide it; that every one is poised to its final place as surely as if angel-hands had set out with it from heaven. Like the kindred host above, God calleth them all by name, and appointeth each its place.

No wind blows but God knows ;
No atom falls but God calls.

The storm looks like riot : it is a kind of quiet.
It looks like chaos : it is perfect cosmos. It
makes us think of chance ; and chance, when we
really think of it, resolves itself into unknown
depths on depths of law !

I have spoken of a few of the treasures which
we careless ones seldom think of as lying hidden
in our common snow : of the gradual preparation
of the seasons for it ; of the beauty of the flakes,
and their variety of forms, and of the identity
running through all that variety ; of their secret
architecture, guessed at, never seen ; of the
power necessary to bring and build the atoms
so ; of the careful glory thus in waiting for all
waters, although the transfiguration may not
outlast an instant ; of the kinship of the ice to
the heaven-spaces ; and of the order in the riot
of the storm. The story would grow long, if we
should try to even hint the *uses* of the snow : to
tell how glaciers have planed and moulded and
ground the continents into readiness for man ;
how the polar snows send us out the air and
water-currents, those mighty vehicles on which
the seasons go riding around the planet ; how
the snow-mountains are the nurseries of the
rivers ; how the winter-lands have been in his-

tory the homesteads of strong, young races, that
from time to time freshened the earth with men;
and how the snow-storms take care of all our
northern vegetation, wrapping it from cold,
while the hidden life within gets ready for its
resurrection.

But all this we pass by. Sight-seeing, as
every traveller knows, is about the hardest
work a man can do. Let us draw ourselves
away, and for a moment think over two or
three thoughts that the treasures thus far seen
arouse of him who is their Lord.

The first thought of all must needs be, — *Then
there is nothing common, nothing trifling, nothing un-wonderful in this universe!* Beauty far
off! Sights in Europe! Why, here, now, all
around us, under our feet, in the air, the weed
springing up unbidden in our flower-pot, the bit
of spar or sea-shell on our mantel-piece, the
paving stone we rattle over, the most familiar,
unsightliest, deadest thing that we can name,
has more of God in it than we can ever see.
Explain it away, and we have only explained
a way through it to deeper marvels beyond.
" Nothing common or unclean!" we may well

say, taught by the wonder of the great sheet, let down, like Peter's in the vision, through the winter air.

Clustered around the old cathedrals abroad, you often see old wooden houses leaning up against the sculptured walls, like ragged children about the knees of a great, beautiful saint. We say well that the shanty is unfair compared with the cathedral. But that is only true so far as man's part is concerned. Look at God's part in each: the wood-cells and fibres in the shanty's walls, grown by the laws of plant-life, show structure even more complex and marvellous than the white crystals built up into the shining temple. Nothing common or unclean!

Truly see the contents of any bit of time or space, and we feel with William Blake that

> "We see a World in a grain of sand,
> And a Heaven in a wild-flower,
> Hold Infinity in the palm of our hand,
> And Eternity in an hour!"

To this thought, that nothing is insignificant when really seen, joins on a second,— of the large place in the universe which the little things hold. Nay, when we think of it, everything resolves itself to littles. Nature is noth-

ing but little things. The mountain becomes
motes of silex and calcium, the ocean single
drops of water, the prairie single grains of
alumina, the human body single cells, human life
single thoughts and feelings and impulses. And
earth, air, fire, water, become, in turn, atoms of
oxygen, hydrogen, nitrogen and the rest. There
is no stopping-place. When you have summed
up what God does by means of his " little things,"
and, for the most part, in utter silence, there
will be nothing left to think of.

The Mahometans have a story that once,
when Abraham had been wronged by the
hunter, Nimrod, Jehovah befriended the patri-
arch, and told him to select the animal that
should be sent to punish his enemy. Abraham
chose the fly. And Jehovah said, " If Abraham
had not chosen the fly, I should have sent a
creature, of whom a thousand would not weigh
as much as a fly's wing."

We often say that God is infinitely great.
We instinctively look up to heaven when we
pray. And doubts often beset us, because, to
our thought, he seems too large and too remote
to be our God,— to care for *me*. That is true:
God is the infinitely great and infinitely remote;

but every whit as truly he is the infinitely little, and so the infinitely close. God the infinitely little! Pray to him! I do not mean that we can find out him; but I think it does help to make us feel that the Great Life is near.

Think of the crystals in which the sap of your trees is lying locked through all this wintry weather,—sap-crystals locked in cells which are themselves invisible to the unaided eye. God stands inside those crystals, holding their atoms fast,—just as much as in the stars!

Think how that sap will be running through the hidden channels next June, and out to the tips of waving leaves, and, in its mimic tides, sweeping round and round the grains of green chlorophyl; so that, when we pluck a leaf and hold it in our hand, we shall really hold a little sea with throbbing life in it. God stands and listens to the dashings of those hidden tides! Does not that help us a little to imagine one who "measures the water in the hollow of his hand," and listens to "the music of the spheres"?

Think of the corpuscles in our human blood, of which it is calculated that seventy billions (some seventy times the population of the globe) lie in a cubic inch:—the Power has counted them! Does it not help a little to make real the thought of One who "sitteth on the circle of the earth, and the inhabitants thereof are as grasshoppers, and the nations as the small dust of the earth; who calleth the stars by names, and not one faileth"?

Or, once more, think of the creatures that play in a single drop of ditch-water as the whales play in the Atlantic. Each one of those creatures has its perfect . structure, its finished anatomy, its instincts and its wants, and those wants provided for, its little hungers and rages, its fatigues and rests, its pains and pleasures, and at last its death,—who knows but its immortality also? Thinking of such things, we begin to feel that perhaps the truth is God is not too far off, but too near for us to see. And God in all, God through all, becomes the living fact.

And the more the universe has widened to us by the aid of those curved bits of glass that we call telescope and microscope, and the more the unknown has become the known, always and everywhere Order, Beauty, Law we find. Always Cosmos, never a sign of Chaos, never an atom fallen out of the All-Ruling Hands!

No chance anywhere, not even in the seeming riot of the storm. No "miracle" anywhere, no breaking of a law; but all a miracle more real by being law. Oneness everywhere! The laws that round the planets rounding the dew-drop: gravitation in the snow-flake's flutter and in the rush of suns. All the recent discoveries and guesses of science are but different paths by which we approach grander points of view, whence we can look and see what it means to say that God is One. This is the unity of Nature, that "one God," to whose recognition the prophets of science are gladly leading us. Oneness from rims to centre of the universe,— rims that are nowhere, centre that is everywhere! And nothing little, nothing trifling; for all is full of God!

It is hard to prove a God; harder to prove him our God; harder still, perhaps, to prove our immortality. Yet a sense as if there were nothing but God everywhere deepens in us, as we enter into the treasures of the snow. Like snow, we, too, become a moment's vision, then we melt and vanish; but I am willing to trust for life and love while I know that the Power and Beauty which moulds the snow-flake is around me and is in me.

Verily, as we watch the white star that has fluttered from the heavens to our hand, we may say, "The Lord is in his holy temple: let our hearts keep silence before him!"

RESURRECTION.

II.

RESURRECTION.

It is the Resurrection season, and the glad word itself shall be our theme to-day. We will simply say it over and over, and listen to the echoes which it raises among our thoughts. It is the word in which the twins, Death and Life, declare themselves to be not two, but one; and the echoes, although vague, must needs be strong and musical, and they will bring us hints from far.

Not all from afar, however: the echo which reaches us first, from the hills and fields, sounds near.

Very beautiful, was it not? that picture of the opening spring-time which I gathered from our Bible, catching here a glimpse and there a glimpse as it lies reflected in the song of psalmist and prophet, and of Jesus, who had so often watched it as a boy on the hills of Galilee. Doubtless he used to go out to gather early lilies and note the green garments of the fresh young grass. Ten million million tiny strug-

glers on our hills and in our fields to-day are
trying to show us that ours, too, is Holy Land.
The flowers have begun to greet us in our walks,
—dumb angels, with faces all a-shine with the
glad tidings that the Savior-season hath arisen.

Winter we call the death of the year. Its
white suggests the shroud; its silence the hush
of the saddened house; its evenness of aspect
the blank uniformity of loss; its cold and voice-
less, yet potent, influence the spell that absence
of things dear and wonted lays on us. Yet to
what a miracle of life does all this tend! The
swathing and the silence and the rest only hide
the inward processes by which the earth, in its
white chrysalis, is preparing itself for motion
and color and sound.

How certain it is, this Resurrection of the
spring! Some one reminds us that, as the harvest approaches, the world is annually within
a month or two of actual starvation. Let one
single spring-time drop from out the roll of
seasons, and another would look on an earth
full of silent cities and very quiet villages, waiting for new populations,— for some provident
Noah to wander by that way and settle with his
family.

How punctual, too! Winter may be cold or warm, may linger or haste away, or turn back and growl us out a snowy good-bye a month after we were thinking he had gone,— but it makes little difference, after all. The heralds soon arrive, and then the gay procession of life marches in in order. We can predict the coming banners, can date the passing weeks by flower-arrivals and departures, can count the quick hours by flower-wakings and flower-closings. Emerson is but a trifle too precise:—

> " The calendar
> Of the painted race of flowers,
> Exact to days, exact to hours,
> Is faithful through a thousand years;
> And the pretty almanac
> Shows the punctual coming back
> On their due days of the birds."

And how nearly universal the Resurrection is! The green tide comes pouring up from the south, pressing over the hills and running through the river-valleys, and presently not one inch that can wear green but is bathed in the living glory. The trees, swelling with buds, set their brown nets in its path, and soon the meshes are full of crinkled leafage and the white and crimson of the blossoms; and mosses wake and steal into their rooty arms, and the vines creep up their bodies. No secret place is left unvisited by Spring. The lone plant in a desert, the seed buried under a dead leaf in the wood or prisoned in the crevice of a city pavement, the stick-dry bush we hung up in the cellar last November out of sight, the very potatoes in the barrel,— all hear the whisper and feel the touch and turn to life again. Within the room of a sick girl, in a foul city-garret, stands a solitary rose in an earthen pitcher, cut off, like a caged bird, from the companionship of kin. The Spring, flying over, knows the spot, stops, and bids the plant and the sick one turn again to life and beauty. She works for no eyes. She works for all eyes. The green deep of the forest, the deep of your little parlor-fernery, turning now to a tropical jungle,— both are alike to her; and all her work is finished with equal exquisiteness.

Where she cannot go in one shape, she startles in another. Here, among us, her presence is an even leafing of the temperate zone, beneath a brightening sun. Northward, closer to the pole, there comes a rapid dash of day and spring and summer all in one, as she watches her chance to fling green among the snows. Elsewhere, it needs a dimming sun to bring her. In inner California, through long, rainless months of heat, the roots and bulbs lie dormant underneath the earth's burnt crust, just as with us they hide beneath the frozen earth of winter, while only thick-rinded, juicy evergreens linger above the desert's surface,— matching the firs and pines amid our snows. There the Resurrection season comes as the coolest of the year. The rain sets in, the desert-crust grows cool and soft, and suddenly, as if the rain had touched them with a magic torch, the plains are lit with color !

In the still drier tropics, she will come, if she can come no other way, down the sun-baked channel of an empty river,— the spring-time that the traveller, Baker, saw far up one of the great branches of the Nile. He tells us how his party had been travelling weary days through the plains of Upper Egypt. Everything was death-stricken with the heat: no grass, no green ; the water of the river had shrunken to little lakes, a mile or two long, lying scattered here and there along the dry bed. And these pools swarmed and throbbed with the concen-

trated life of the big river; the fish, the croco-
diles and hippopotamuses crowding there together in unhappy families. One night, when
the men were camped as usual in the sandy
channel, he heard a dull and distant noise. It
grew loud and louder. It woke the Arabs up,
who knew the sound and sprang to their feet
shouting, "The river! The river!" and scram-
bled for the banks. And then they heard the
River come,—marching down through the night
on its journey to the sea! When the morning
broke, a yellow flood, hundreds of yards across,
rolled at their feet in what at night had been
a dry and sunken pathway through the desert.
Far away, up in the mountains, the rainy season
had begun, and thus sent greeting to the plains.
In two days, the face of the whole country had
changed around the travellers. Water was all
that the solitary place needed to make it blossom like a garden. The mimosa-trees budded
on the banks, the birds found their way with
singing to the branches, the deer came down in
companies to drink, the green spread and deep-
ened like a dye; and it was spring!

Thus, everywhere, in one form or another,—
under ground, dissolving minerals for the suck-

ing rootlets,—mounting through a million secret tubes inside young stems and solid trees,— descending from the skies in sunshine and in showers,— riding on the rivers,— comes Spring, the Savior-season in the gladness of the Resurrection.

We will turn from the fields and listen to another echo of that word,— one that comes from the heavens that bend above them. What *makes* this miracle of spring? Where does the spring-*force* come from? And whither go, when the leaves drop and the flowers pass away? How explain this steady swing of seasons by which alternate life and death sweep like a rising, then an ebbing, tide over the planet, so certainly, so punctually, so universally?

In Greece, six hundred years before Christ's day, still earlier farther east, wise men perceived something like the truth, that matter and force are eternal, that the words "creation" and "annihilation" have no meaning. They said that something never comes from nothing, never ends in nothing; and they framed philosophies accordingly. But for ages this remained a philosopher's idea. Not till within a century of our own time have the chemists proved by experiments with weight and measure that no atom of matter is ever really lost; that everything which vanishes only vanishes from *sight*, to enter into new combinations and exist as truly as before. And not till within the last few years has another fact begun to secure its proof,—that not only what we call "matter" is thus indestructible, but also what we call "force" is imperishable; since heat and light, electricity and magnetism, chemic and vital force, are all of them but varying forms of one and the same great force. The "correlation of forces,"—so its discoverers have named the mighty secret which at last reveals to us the depths of meaning in man's old word, "uni-verse." Correlated forces,—that is to say, *each one dies into the others when it disappears as itself:* one sole Force abiding as the "I AM." In uttering that, we stand in the very heart, the inmost miracle, of the Resurrection process!

Take any common movement that we have ceased to wonder at, thinking we know all about it; trace it back and see the dyings of force from one form and its rebirths in another. You have a clock on the mantel-piece in your parlor. Whence get the hands of the clock their motion? From the force of gravitation in the leaden weights or of elasticity in the steel spring. Whence came that force into the weights or spring? Out of your contracting muscles as they wound it up. So the power is already outside of the clock, and in your arm. Whence came this vital, muscular force into your arm? It is the chemic force that lurked in the beef you eat for dinner. The butcher and the baker brought it to you, the farmer sent it. And before it was you, that meat was ox; before it was ox, it was grass; before it was grass, it was mineral in the earth, and gas in the air, and water. But what so marvellously wrought up the chemic force in gas and mineral to chemic force in me? The sun's heat did it! Nay, that chemic force, it is supposed, is itself the sun's ray, transformed from the power that darts through space to that which holds the atoms of the elements fast-locked together. Somewhat thus the men of science tell the story. The busy creeping of the clock's hands round their little circle is traced out of the clock, out of me who wind it up, out of the food that made me, out of the earth which produced the food, back, back, to the great time-measurer in the heavens. The sun winds up our watches! And whence got the sun its heat? Perhaps by the constant condensation of its vast body, possibly by the striking of vast hordes of whirling meteors on its surface. Both theories may be doubted, and be supplanted by new theories; but, on any theory, we have now to follow our clock's creep beyond our sun to the vast interstellar spaces where the world-systems gather themselves together from nebulæ, and myriads of suns charm their planets to attentive courses.

Is it not very wonderful? Forever and forever,— there is no stopping in the vast journey, if we ask the wherefore of the simplest motion that our eyes perceive. Nothing wasted, nothing lost; each particle accounted for ; each pulse of light or heat or electricity forever doing its appointed work in ceaseless resurrections; at each birth exactly reproducing in new forms that which had ceased in old ones.

And, if we could watch with eyes all-seeing, we should expect to watch those world-systems themselves coming and going like the leaves upon our trees, like the human generations,— systems evolving, and dissolving, and then again evolving, in endless cycles of cosmic reproduction.

Such is the great Resurrection Psalm which modern science reverently sings. We find its noble verse in such chapters as Tyndall and Spencer write. To go back, then, to the fields and answer our question, What makes the spring-force? That which is true of the clock upon the mantel is but more magnificently true of our spring-time on the earth. The motion of our May, vast as it is and beautiful, is but a little stir in the eternal Resurrection process by which the sun mothers all motion on the earth. A little more, a little less of sunlight,— that is all that makes the play of seasons. The earth, in its round, places itself so that the rays fall more vertically on its surface, and the deed is done! Only that and nothing more, and, lo! the south winds blow; the rivers run; the frozen ground turns into flowers; the trees break forth at every inch into leaf-life; the pilgrim birds arrive, singing and mating; the children are shouting in the street; the young men and maidens are marrying; the old people are thanking God that the rheumatism has left their bones; the poor are easy and hopeful again; the armies are moving; the wars begin again; and all the comedies and tragedies of plant and animal and human life are in full play once more. Sun's heat,— that is all that has done it! And each transformation of the force, from the time it issues from the sun in lightning thrills to the time it quickens the pulsing of a sick child's blood, or stirs as nerve-force in the cells of the poet's brain,— what is it but a vanishing to reappear, a dying into a Resurrection?

Let us leave the world of fields and skies, and enter that of man. Here, if we speak our word and listen, it will echo for us from every part of human experience.

We hear it grandly in the fate of nations. One blots out another by conquest, then that vanisher rises again by the slow absorption of its civilization. The old cultures of the race are thus secured and handed down in cycles of rhythmic history. Hebrew absorbs Canaanite, and Persia absorbs Babylon, Egypt and Asia Minor and Persia yield to Greece, and Greece to Rome, and Rome to barbarous Goth and Frank; and throughout the process Man saves his own, and the forces, mental and moral, are guided to the finer issues of modern Europe and America. The brains that planned the pyramids, the bravery of the warriors at Troy, the enthusiasm of the Crusader, are hoarded in the broadened intellect and nobler ideals and fairer instincts of the children of to-day.

We hear another echo, another series of echoes, repeated from every individual life. *One* death we die? Why, we die from one day to another. We only live by dying. The doctors say our very bodies are changed, atom by atom, every few years; that you are not quite the same persons you were when you met here the last time. And do not all mothers know what it is to lose their children's faces, not by a death-day, but by the swift birthday circling round?

In mind, in character, who doubts our fact? A young man grasps, at last, the real purpose of his life, a girl leaves her school and enters on home duties; what is that but a dying of the boy and girl, a Resurrection to the man, the woman? Then, perhaps, they awake to the feeling that they are living lives of busy selfishness and uselessness and sin; and with deep heart-

searching and repenting, with prayer and vow
and earnest struggle, they consecrate themselves
to something better. It is the fairest of all the
Resurrections,— a dying of the poor self, a rising
to the nobler self. Friends well name it the
revival, the new birth.

Half-way between their birthday and their
death-day, this man and this woman stand side
by side before the minister. They call it " wed-
ding-day ": it is their Resurrection-day! What
dies? Two separate selves. Two separate
homes, that now are breaking up. What comes
to birth? Two lives in one. A new home. A
new family. A new starting-point for births
and deaths, for joys and tragedies, for obedience to laws of love and life, and nobler
growth thereby, or for breaking of those laws
and thereby growing ruin. Can they fully
know, these two, the solemn act of Life-in-Death
in which they join, so brimful with consequence?
Not they!

While they are finding out, the years pass on,
and our man and woman are, once more, two,—
for one of them is here, one gone. And again
there is a Resurrection to be watched. A voice
is gone, yet, hark! its tones are " rising " in those

children's voices ringing out at play. A smile is gone; yet there it lurks around the fresh young lips and eyes. The pose of the head, the motion of the body, the habits of the hands still linger in the home. The mother or the father is dead, but the mother's love or the father's honor has "risen" in the form of family-ideals to shape new lives of gentle deeds and manly ways.

Is it ever otherwise? We read of Theodore Parker, that, as he lay on his death-bed in Florence, in a wandering mood he grasped the hand of a friend, and said eagerly: "I have something to tell you: there are two Theodore Parkers now. One is dying here in Italy; the other I have planted in America. He will live there and finish my work." Many a wanderer from the beaten creed-paths has found that "other" Parker sown through the wide land, and blessed the risen messenger that showed him God afresh. I think it is never otherwise. Truly, the chemists of history cannot weigh and count and prove; but, seeing what we do of the laws of Life-in-Death, we have a faith to say that in the world of mind, as in that of matter, Nature gathers up the fragments so that nothing is

lost,— no thought or feeling or ideal perish-
ing utterly, any more than atoms or vibrations
physical.

But there is borne to us, thinking of such vanished friends, one echo more, the most mys-
terious of all. Let us listen to it quietly and
reverently.

Ah ! if we could interpret that word " Resurrection " *fully*, and not in dim, far hints, we
should fathom the depths of consciousness and
unconsciousness. " Birth " and " Death " would
be new words to us ; not events of beginning
and ending, but instants in an eternal process
of Becoming. If we could interpret that word
fully, it would explain not only the mystery
beyond, but that mystery which is past. We
should find out the whence and the how of this
body's Resurrection to its *present* form. Where
was our body

> " In the beautiful repose
>   That it had *before its birth*,
> With the ruby, with the rose,
>   With the harvest, earth in earth " ?

How came it that our dust was not the ruby,
was not rose, was not part of some golden har-

vest ? How came it that, when we rose, we rose as baby-man and baby-woman, as Nellie, John and Willie ?

"The Soul that rises with us, our life's Star,
    Hath had elsewhere its setting,
        And cometh from afar."

O that we had some angel of the Resurrection to tell us what we were in the immortality that lies behind us! And how we came from that to this; what death we died to reach this life; what forgotten pains we have passed through, and what joys; and how much of that old experience we have brought with us! Have we, buried in us, like the trees, rings of many seasons of rebirths and redeaths? And does our hope of immortality lie rooted in a memory? Is the seed's dream of the flower it will be a dim consciousness of blossom-tints that *have* enfolded it, and of free winds it once knew upon the tree-top? Have we come up, or come down, to this new life on earth; been some time more than we are now; and are we limping Lucifers fallen by some prenatal sin to human incarnation, or stand we now upon the topmost step of being we have ever touched? Are we as wakers to our past, and is *that* the reason

that it lies so vague and dim? Are we as
sleeping dreamers to our future, and is that the
reason that *it* lies so dim? Are we always
passing from a night into a morning, which is
still but night to the brighter days that lie beyond? It is question upon question, and no
answer! At least, the only angels that give
answer are this same curious mind in us that
asks the question,— this thirsting aspiration to
be yet more,— this love that clings,— this sense
of duty that seems as if it never could be born
and never die, but always must have been to
always be,— this inward voice of "Life! Life!"
that haunts us so forever. No answer more
than that.

But, I think, it helps us, in doubts we have
about our future life, to remember how almost
completely the two mysteries are one,— that
which shrouds the Resurrection which has been
at birth to make us what we are, and that
around the Resurrection that shall be. Solve
the first, and you have solved the last. Nay,
tell me *what I am* to-day, and you have probably solved both. The deep secret is not the
secret of the future, but the secret of becoming
one thing from having been another. Deeper

yet, the mystery of *being* at all. But that "becoming one thing from having been another,"— it is the common mystery of growth. The processes which we cease to wonder at because they go on all the time under our eyes, by which a few pounds of soft and winking babyhood become the Napoleon or Daniel Webster who shape the nations; these processes by which we differ to-day from what we were when the last flowers were in the fields,— are part of that same miracle of growth, of becoming, of which birth and death, whatever they may be, are certainly but other parts. We can trace the process, one little inch of it. But that is a wholly different thing from explaining even that inch. If I could but *explain* myself as I am, or the difference between myself of to-day and myself of yesterday, I should doubtless have a stronger argument for my immortality than any that the thinkers yet have framed.

Why do we, then, concentrate our wonder on one moment in the horizon of our time-view, and sorrowfully call that narrowed wonder "doubt about our immortality"? Look behind, and explain the moment when you rose on the verge of the horizon in that direction.

A daily, momently rising has made us the beings that now stand in our footprints. That
instantly recurring Resurrection will go on till,
again, what they call *us* will go below the straining vision of our friends. And what then?
Why comes then the doubt for the first time
with a startling horror, "What if there be no
resurrection of the dead?" Nay: standing
amid the greatness of this Resurrection thought,
we begin to feel, in spite of all our ignorance,
that there is no meaning in that word "dead!"
*Nothing in death can be stranger than every-
thing in life.* The "argument" for all we want
in immortality is unattaining: it falls far short
of the questions to which we long to have an
answer. But nearly every man who thinks
amid his trust, and yet knows that he does
trust and is happy amid his thinking, comes
probably to two convictions as his final state-
ments,— this for one: All of me there is, has
ever been, and all will ever be, each atom and
each impulse of me, whatever new form atom
or impulse take. And this, too, one feels sure
of with a mighty sureness,— that the facts about
that unknown future form, whatever they may
be, lie within the Eternal Goodness, and are,

therefore, surely better than our best hope about them. My brightest hope is ignorance still. My trust in Goodness — to me that does not seem like ignorance. That trust, and the Resurrection at my birth, so strange, so unremembered, hinting at so much life unknown behind, are, as it were, God's affidavit that I need not fear about the Resurrections to come.

Thank God, then, friends, for the Resurrection thoughts which the spring months bring to us! We die to live again. We die *that we may* live again. Nothing is quickened save it die. Mortality is the condition of all immortality. What echoes we have wakened of this truth! The opening spring prints it off on every hillside in illuminated text of leaf and flower. The suns in the heaven are blazing it. The nations in their history repeat it. The sin-experience in which we first find God reveals it. The passing moment of each man's and woman's life is ringing gladly with it. Our dead friend's memory recalls it. The mystery of each instant's life flashes it far backward through the past, far forward through the future. We find, as always with these central facts of Nature, that the best and

highest meaning of the truth belongs to ourselves,— so completely is Man a part of all, so
completely is all represented in Man. Our word
"Resurrection" seems to concentrate the history
of the universe, to whisper the secret of the
life of God!

And as we think of all these things, those
words which I read you awhile ago fill and throb
with their tides of meaning : —

Praise ye the Lord, all things that *die!* Ye
die that ye may live again.

Praise ye him, sun and moon, that yet shall
fade!

Praise him all ye stars of light, whose light
shall yet be quenched!

Praise the Lord, O earth, so full of changing
deaths! Praise him, fire and hail, snow and
vapors, and stormy winds, each vanishing as ye
fulfil his word!

Praise him, mountains and all hills, that yet
shall melt!

Praise him, beasts and all birds! Praise him,
young men and maidens, old men and children!
Let everything that hath the breath of life
praise the Lord ; for all shall die, *that all may
live again!*

Praise *ye* the Lord!

FLOWERS.

III.

FLOWERS.

" Consider the lilies, how they grow," said Jesus; " they toil not, they spin not,— yet Solomon in all his glory was not arrayed like one of these."

One summer day I happened into a flower exhibition. A placard gave notice that the subject of the day's discussion was to be "The Lily"; and relying on the word of Jesus as a pass, I went in obediently to hear the garden-men "consider the lilies, how they grow." The Japan lily was the special subject of the talk: how could the stranger best be made to grow among ourselves? One man told of his greenhouse luck, and another of his pot-luck, and the next one talked of soils, and so on, round the circle. And all the while the superb things stood upon their stalks and looked at us, no king in all his glory arrayed like one of them !

That word of Jesus is almost the only tender

word about flowers in all the Bible. In the
books of the Apocrypha and in the Song of Solomon, roses and lilies are mentioned twice or
thrice in the lover's way; but the Hebrew feeling for Nature was rather a feeling of its sub-
limity than of its beauty. The sun and stars,
the mountains and the desert and the sea, the
rains, the lightning and the earthquake, these
stand forth in the Old Testament imagery. And
trees were loved, and fruit was praised. But
grass and leaves are scarcely spoken of save as
the emblem of withering,—"All flesh is grass,"
"We all do fade as a leaf." When the Hebrew
thought of fragrance, he thought of myrrh and
frankincense rather than of roses; and when he
thought of beauty, a gem rather than a blossom
was the wonder to his eye. Many a flash of
ruby and sapphire and emerald gleams from the
Bible pages. The wall of the New Jerusalem
is built up of them, and its twelve gates are
twelve pearls. In that city is a tree of life, and
it has twelve fruits indeed,—but never a word
of flowers in the heaven on earth that was to be.
Paul was too earnest in his gospel of repentance,
and too deep in the revelation of the mystery of
the love of God in Christ to think of the love of

God to the hillsides and the good news revealed
in wild-flowers. So this little word of Jesus
stands almost alone to make us know that there
was, at least, one pair of eyes in Palestine that
saw the Father everywhere. It is one of the
verses that show that Jesus was no common
man.

Yet Jesus "considered" the outside beauty
only, I suppose. Those garden-men I spoke of,
who knew of the tireless toil by which the plant-
cells are built up from the soil, and the wondrous spinning of plant-fibres, and the secret
weddings of the flowers, were considering mysteries of growth of which he could not have
dreamed. Who loved the lily best? Those
who know its wonder best can love it best, no
doubt; and so, I trust, the garden-men. Yet
that were only possible, if the other love, the
Jesus-love, the poet's, the worshipper's love, were
joined to their science. No worship like the
worship of science when it does worship!

What would summer be without the flowers!
And yet a summer with flowers is a modern im-
provement. For ages and ages, through far the
greater part of its life thus far, a flowerless earth

has turned its sombre face up to the sun. It had not learned to smile. Even the summers of the ages to which we owe our coal-beds had no flowers, no fruit-blossoms, no grass, and, of course, no bees and no song-birds in them! All the plants, the wise men say, were like our ferns or club-mosses or meadow-horsetails,— only "there were giants in those days,"— or else like our cone-bearing trees; all reproducing in the secret way the ferns still know, or the quiet way the pine-cones have. Not till long ages afterwards did the Junes bear blossoms.

Thinking of that, we can hardly say "the good old times!" We thank Heaven that the birds and flowers came before us. Indeed, the earth had to be ripe for them before it could be ripe for us. So here we are to-day, and the whole land, all the summer through, laughs for us in grass and flowers,— that peal beginning in anemones and violets, rising into roses, and ending in the golden-rod and asters. Great tribes of beings have been already born, and others are on their way to being, to people the planet with color and beauty.

What place on it shall have the fairest? Where will the Great Gardener walk and work most fondly? On the broad stretches of prairie-floor, paved with gay mosaic? Or in the secret places of the woods? Or on the tiny farms that hardly seem to dot the New England landscape, although Massachusetts is the crowded corner of America? No, none of these,— for Dr. Hayes (was it?) says he never saw such beautiful wild-flowers as in the Arctic zone, where the summer is almost counted by the hours! And Ruskin, with his mountain-love, claims the noblest for the uplands. The grass grows nowhere softer and greener than on the Alpine pastures, or in the glacier meadows of our own Sierras, meadows set nine thousand feet above sea-level; and right out of the Swiss glaciers, nestled by eternal snows, spring rocks whose bright tops are gardens of anemones and gentians. But the lovers of the ocean, meanwhile, tell us that nowhere do the colors glow and deepen so, as where the sea-winds feed them. The reddest wild roses I ever saw grew out of the graves of the old Puritan ministers of Marblehead, who lie in a row among the rocks of the quiet, seaward burying-ground. Or what think you of the great central plain of California in flower-time? For six months of the year

it is a scorched and dust-swept desert. In April
it becomes one flower-bed, nearly four hundred
miles long and thirty wide, lying at the feet of
the snow-mountains. A traveller writes of it:
" Go where I would, east, west, north, south, I
still plashed and rippled in flower-gems. More
than a hundred flowers touched my feet at every
step, closing above them as if I were wading in
water." To count the riches, he gathered the
harvest of one square yard of the plain, taken
at random like a cupful of water from a lake;
and it gave more than seven thousand distinct
flower-heads, besides one thousand stems of
silky grasses,— these rising from an inch-deep
velvet floor, containing, by estimate, a million of
the tiny cups and hoods that we call mosses!

And what a marvel is each one of all the
myriad millions in its individual make and stature! Think what the mathematics of the leaf-
arrangement imply,— that every leaf on every
budding tree in each whole spring is set in its
place by law! that not one has stumbled to
its twig, or to its station on the twig, by any
accident! and that this same ordered stationing
is traceable all through the close phalanx of the
pine-cone's scales, and determines where the

limbs shall start on every tree, and the very
spot within the blossom where each stamen shall
droop or nod !

These last words, linking leaves, limbs and
blossoms, touch the deepest flower-secret that
has thus far been discovered. The school-boys
know it now, but the wisest men were just
knowing enough a century ago to guess it. It
is the secret that the botanists call "metamor-
phosis,"— the secret that each and every organ
of the flower is but a transformed leaf; that
bud-scale and bract and sepal and petal and
stamen and pistil, back to the new bud-scale, in
spite of all the difference of their forms and all
their varied tints, are but successive *leaf-trans-
figurations*. Economic Nature gets her new
effects, not by selecting new themes, but by
playing variations on the old themes; when she
would make a blossom on an apple-tree or on a
pasture-weed, she only shortens and alters what
would else have been a common leafy branch.
How do we know this? By tracing the cousinship of each pair of neighbor organs through
graded series of transitional forms; by watching the conversion and the reconversion of these
organs into each other in domesticated double

flowers; by studying the cases of monstrosity that so often blab Nature's riddles and reveal the latent tendencies of beings: on such full evidence as this we know it.

But, not content with such transfiguration, the Mother of all beauty takes up the separate organs, and tenderly carries out her variations on each one. She bears fixed laws in mind and never really forgets her arithmetic,— the rules of twos and threes and fours and fives; but by multiplying parts, by dividing parts, by joining them at this place on their edges, then at that, by enlarging some and making others smaller, by their complete abortion sometimes, by moulding horns and cups, by unfurling wings, by hanging bells, by ravelling fringes out, by all sorts of dainty devices of sculpture, she makes the myriad distinct species of miracles that men stare at untiringly as the flowers of spring. It is rare luck, in some classic land, to turn up from the soil the fragment of a marble statue of old beauty. But Nature flings her carvings everywhere,— each one complete and fresh and perfect for its niche, and such a joy that, were it the lone one of its race, it would draw the people into pilgrimages for its worship.

She paints them, too. If any one seem ugly as a whole, place a bit of it under the microscope, and see what firmaments of color, what mines of sparkling gems, you have burst into. Under the lens, a quarter-inch of rosy petal flushes and spreads like a sunset sky! A mottled streak turns into a glorious sunrise! You can think of nothing else for fit comparison. And then, instead of voice, she gives them fragrance. They have no speech or language; but in this way their music "goes forth through all the earth and their words to the end of the world." Unless, indeed, Huxley's fancy be fact, and by ears fine enough (possibly only insect-fine) a voice, also, could be heard,—the music of running sap, sound such as streams have that run through secret channels. If so, what choruses rise through all the fields that some one hears!

But what is all this lavish sculpture and painting and fragrance for,—lavished on the waste, where no man is, as well as in the garden-bed; lavished on the blossom's inmost slopes and curves, where human eyes cannot detect it, as much as on the inch of outward surface? We

used to account for it as sign of God's delight
in beauty in itself. We used to say,

> " If eyes were made for seeing,
> Then Beauty is its own excuse for being."

But to-day, again, brings forward a new and
richer thought, that all this beauty and fragrance
is but a path to use. We can plainly see that
all the energy of the plant goes to secure reproduction, that all the parts of the flower subserve
the purpose of seed-making. Deep hidden within the flower's heart lies the little nursery where
the seeds are to be born; most cunningly the
pistil and the stamen watch each other like true
lovers for a greeting; tenderly the petals close
around them in the cool, and open through fit
hours of sunlight. And when the stamens and
the pistil cannot meet directly, but the message
must be borne by insect rovers, then the compli-
cation of contrivance to secure the transport of
the message almost exceeds belief. The pollen
must be brought from a certain spot in one
flower and left on a certain spot within another. Says one, speaking of Darwin's investi-
gation of the orchids: "'Moth-traps and spring-
guns set on these grounds' might well be the
motto of these flowers. There are channels

of approach along which the nectar-loving insects are surely guided, so as to compel them to pass the given spots; there are adhesive plasters nicely adjusted to fit their probosces or to catch their brows, and so unload their pollen-burden; sometimes, where they enter for the honey, there are hair-triggers carefully set in their necessary path, communicating with explosive shells that project the pollen-stalks with unerring aim upon their bodies." And now Darwin adds to his explanations the thought (it is not yet wholly proved, but it is well advanced in proof) that the lustrous colors of the flowers and their rich odors are also contrivances to aid in the reproduction. He has found it " an invariable rule that flowers fertilized by the wind never have the gayly-colored petals," and draws the inference that the beauty and the fragrance come upon the blossoms by long processes of natural selection, because attractive to the insects that are needed to assist in fertilizing them. The colors and the songs of birds and insects, he thinks, are in part similarly brought about. And thus all that gives the life and motion and peculiar gladness to the fields in summer would be literally but the deep inbreathing of the spirit of Love in Nature. How far down it goes, to touch the whole planet to grace and beauty! The thought lifts the rims of our vision and gives to Love a glory of meaning that we never guessed before. It seems to make real our feeling that a Father's heart is beating in all things.

And in this distinction of sex the plants lay hold of us. They come between the mineral and animal kingdoms as the connecting link. For plants not only exercise the primitive digestion,— feeding on minerals, which they organize into the food on which we higher creatures live; they not only hint, while they prepare, our respiration,— draining clear the air of that which poisons us, and restocking it with that which we must breathe; but, in this distinction of sex in their flowers, they rise to the height of their stature and foreshadow the third great function of animal life, that of reproduction. Of the whole plant, the flower is the part nearest akin to us. Like us, it breathes oxygen and gives out carbonic acid. Like us, it therefore gives out heat,—the flower is the hottest part of the plant. Like us, it has rest — seasons,— sleep, so called; and for reproduction needs to

hoard, and, in the process, exhausts vitality.
And, like animals, plants have ancestry and
cousinship, and can only be arranged in a true
system when we arrange them physiologically.

"Consider the lilies," said Jesus. When we
"consider" them and find such thoughts as
these awaiting us, the words of another poet
seem to rhyme across the centuries to his: —

> "Flower in the crannied wall,
> I pluck you out of the crannies,—
> Hold you here, root and all, in my hand,
> Little flower; but if I could understand
> What you are, root and all, and all in all,
> I should know what God and man is!"

But I must leave the flowers themselves to
speak a word about man's love of flowers. The
love declares itself in many ways.

The Arabs, passing a rich harvest-field or a
tree in full bloom, will greet it with a "Barak
Allah!" "May God bless you!" That hints
the world-wide feeling. And the Arab beggars
name their children Ruby, Diamond, Lily, Rose,
and Jessamine. So still do we. Gems and
flowers,— each the highest product of its kingdom, for a gem is the exquisiteness of flint or
clay, and flower the transfiguration of the plant,

—instinctively we take them to name all other things precious and beautiful.

We place the pots, like traps to catch the sunbeams, at our windows, and like to set creation going in our parlors. We make believe at "woods" in little ferneries. We concentrate the fields in our gardens, and the climates in our green-houses. In southern France there are flower-farms. The Flower Mission to the hospitals and prisons is the daintiest form of modern loving-kindness. The Horticultural Society in Boston holds a Saturday morning worship all through the summer, and it is better than cathedral-joy to linger at its altars. In England, the rich people have established Flower Exhibitions for workingmen. The little gardens that furnish the display are window-ledges in the back streets of London, or a box upon the roof-top, or little plots, six feet by ten, before the door. A boy will bring his solitary geranium, a girl her carnation, the father has his one or two rare roses (perhaps the money that bought them was saved from the ale-house), whose every leaf-bud has made breakfast-talk and after-supper watchings for the family. Each competing pot must have its seal and knot of ribbon. And, when the day arrives, the lords and ladies come and look and praise, and then the sixpenny admission lets in the eager, well-dressed crowd,— and all get prizes, I believe; and the factory-hands go home deciding what flower they will train to enter at the next annual show. The factory-hand's life holds room for that!

Love has made many lovers foolish; but it took flower-love to drive a nation crazy. And of all nations it was the sober-headed Dutchmen! Once in Holland they grew ecstatic over tulips; so crazily fond of tulips that two thousand dollars was cheap for a certain bulb. All ranks, high and low, were carried off their understandings into tulip-speculations; the towns had their tulip-exchange; the public notary became the tulip-notary. And when the bubble burst, fortunes vanished, the panic was national, and the country did not get over the shock to its commerce for several years.

In other ways than this of cultivation, the ancient love has shown itself. Art has fed itself on flowers. Architecture tells the story earliest. The heavy Egyptian column imitates, it is supposed, the palm-tree's trunk, and its capital the

lotus-bud of the Nile. The Corinthian capital
is the acanthus-leaf. The stones of Gothic architecture conspire in a hundred forms to imi-
tate the vegetable structure.

Poetry is full of flower-fields, because each
flower seems full of poetry to us. The flower-
names are often little poems in themselves. Those
long, uncouth names, dreaded in botany, hide
Nature-meanings in them. Heliotrope is "she
who turns to the sun"; mesembryanthemum is
"flower of the mid-day"; nasturtium carries its
meaning of "bent-nose" in its face; geranium
is "crane's-bill," — let the seed-vessel grow and
it will tell the reason why; saxifrage is "rock-
cleaver," named so from its birthplace in the
clefts; anemone is "wind-flower." These, you
see, were but simple heart and eye names to
the Greeks or Romans, just as we call the pets
heart's-ease, day's-eye, morning-glory, honey-
suckle, mignonette. Each people has its own.
Other flower-names come down to us impearled
with myth and story,— the hyacinth, narcissus,
Solomon's - seal, arethusa, the passion - flower.
What sacred romances the lotus-flower, the mar-
tyr's palm, the victor's laurel, recall! There
is probably no famous poet that has not sealed

his fame into a song about some favorite of the fields. Wordsworth's celandines and daffodils are noted, and Burns's daisy, and Herbert's rose, and Emerson's rhodora, and Lowell's dandelion; while in Chaucer the whole spring buds and sings, and all along the lines of Tennyson flowers brush you with fine touches.

Nay, every one plays poet with them, although he write no verses. We use them to interpret all the tenderest things in life. When the lovers want to tell the unutterable words, they betake themselves to the dumb messengers who have learned to say so much. When we want to remember a hill-top view, a meeting that has made a holiday, some spot holy with old history, we pluck a flower to hold the memory fast. When we want to send the home-presence tangibly in a letter, a flower from the window or the field close by will carry it best. Old books drop out the faded blossoms, put there "to mark great places with due gratitude." The California miner caught sight of the mountain heart's-ease just where his uplifted pick was going to fall, and, ere it fell, he was at home across the continent, and in his own pasture where, a barefoot boy, he drove the cows a thousand times. Hollyhocks and lilacs,— who thinks of them, and does not see a quiet country dooryard in the sunshine? The sick soldiers in army hospitals, longing for certain faces, tones and touches, greeted the flowers as the best substitute. "Now, I've got something for you!" said a woman-nurse, holding the bunch behind her, to a very sick New England soldier, "something for you, just like what grows in your front dooryard at home. Guess!" "Lalocs!" he whispered; and she laid them on his folded hands. "O lalocs! how did you know that?" The lilacs outlived him.

Flowers and Art; flowers and Poetry; we must add,— the flowers and *Science.* For in the flowers a name is written, and to-day that name is found to have been written from the beginning in all things that are. All things *grow.* The flower is type of the universe, and the lily of the field is solving afresh for us the problems of creation :—

> We linger at the vigil
>   With him who bent the knee
> To watch the old-time lilies
>   In distant Galilee;

And still the worship deepens
  And quickens into new,
As, brightening down the ages,
  God's secret thrilleth through :
The flower-horizons open !
  The blossom vaster shows !
We hear the wide worlds echo,—
  " See how the lily grows ! "

Nature shows us the world-systems "growing,"—growing from the nebula through æons of gaseous and fluid toward the solid state; shows our earth "growing" from its naked chaos up to the beauty of man's present dwelling-place; shows life on the earth "growing" through uncouth forms and dim sensations up to the beauty of man's stature and the miracle of human brain. Not "creation" anywhere, but evolution; not manufacture, but growth; not inbreaking miracles, but steadfast forces of transfiguration moving all things on by law not a God decreeing from without, but the Living Power within each and all things, "working hitherto."

History shows us thought and morals "growing" from beast-likeness up to all we hail as most divine, most "personal." No "pause in history" at such eras as the origin of Chris-

itanity,— no halt and then an " origin," at all,—
no sudden grace of "revelation " injected then
into human borders; but Man upon those
Mediterranean shores slowly ripening amid the
change of empires and religions, until the recognition of God's fatherhood and men's brother-
hood and the god-likeness of self-sacrifice for
others, came as natural blossoms on the stem
of time.

And consciousness reveals the flower-law in
the processes of personal salvation. The sin-
ner " grows " toward the saint, as he tries and
fails and tries again from day to day; heaven
is a gradual winning, not a surprise of giving;
the kingdom of heaven comes not *to* the earth,
but comes *on* the earth by " growing " there;
and the prayer " Thy will be done! " can blossom to an answer only as each one " grows " to
do the will: —

> Shy yearnings of the savage,
>   Unfolding, thought by thought,
> To holy lives are lifted,
>   To visions fair are wrought;
> The races rise and cluster,
>   And evils fade and fall,
> Till chaos blooms to beauty,
>   God's purpose crowning all!

And so the flower-love, mounting through art, poetry, science, shows itself in man's *worship* also. Thought seldom rises more naturally up to God than when it rises from bending over flowers. In Buddhist lands, they long have been the choicest offering that man brings to the altar. As we keep the Christ's birthday with evergreens, the east keeps the Buddha's with blossoms; and when his tomb was opened two hundred years after his burial, the funeral flowers were found more fragrant and more exquisite than ever, we are told. There are holy blossoms there that symbolize the sun, the world, the throne of God,— flower-symbols as sacred to millions as is the cross to Christians. *We* bring the flowers into our churches: like music visible, they fill the pauses in the service; and who comes here with purer face or -life of sweeter obedience to the laws of Nature?

So sweet, so pure, they are, that, like our holiest friends, they fit not joy and wedding moments only, but still more naturally they come in amid the tragedies, the silences, the heart-breaks. Is not this the reason why?—

"When heaven grows dim, and faith seeks to renew
  The image of its everlasting dower,
 I know no argument so sweet as through
  The bosom of a flower.—

> " A wicket-gate to heaven (of which Death
>   Is the grand portal, sealed to mortal eyes),
> Between whose little bars there comes the breath
>   Of airs from Paradise."

When the " grand portal" has opened and
shut close to us, and we are left with straining
gaze outside, the " wicket-gate " seems to give
comfort. It seems to grant some little vision
into the hidden heart of things, suggesting that
the darkness everywhere holds possibilities better even than our hopes. Save for the flower-
fact, who could have dreamed that such beauty
lurked in the dark earth, was latent in the tiny
seed? So we place the flowers around the still,
cold face; we lay them on our soldiers' graves;
we bring them to the sick-room and the bedside
of·the dying; and everywhere, after words fail
and even music hushes, their presence is a voice-
less, unconfuted argument that the Power within
all silences and pains and tragedies is Love, and
that the possibilities of life are infinite.

THE HARVEST-SECRET.

IV.

THE HARVEST-SECRET.

WHAT is a Harvest-Season?

It is Death — but a Fruition. It is stripped trees, but barrelled apples; stubble in the field, but wheat at the mill; out-of-doors, a naked world, the summer-things all gone, empty nests clinging to the boughs, brown leaves swinging their last hour in the wind or rustling crisply under foot; and, indoors, thanksgiving season for the populations saved again, and for glad homes nestling closer.

The dying of our leaves was predetermined long ago, as all deaths are, in the very constitution of their frames. The earthy minerals that mingle in the sap and climb the tree, unable to evaporate, have to halt up in the tree-top; and there they pack the leaf-cells, until these lose their power to vitalize the sap. But, by the time this happens, it is October and the fruit is made; and the leaves, their first use over, are nearly ready for a second,— to play the part of little carriers, and bear their pack of minerals back into the ground. Almost as soon as they appeared in spring, this moment was foreseen and preparation made for it. Where the leaf-stalk joins the twig, a ring of thick cells began to grow across from outside inwards and bar the entrance of the sap,— sealing beforehand what would else have been a wound upon the twig, and at last leaving the leaf so loosely held that the pat of any wandering breeze will push it off. Presently, but not until the fruition-deed is done, the fateful breeze arrives; and the leaves, faithful unto death to the Lord of the Harvest, go where good leaves go,—

"Where the rain may rain upon them,
Where the sun may shine upon them,
Where the wind may sigh upon them,
And the snow may die upon them,"—

there, even in death, to minister to the beauty of new leaves that are to be. And as they cease from their higher use, Beauty, the reward of Use comes over them: their colors turn the hill-sides around New England villages into walls like the New Jerusalem's,— that city of clear gold, whose wall was garnished with all precious stones.

Fruition and a Death. That does not mean success becoming failure, then. The dying is part of the success. The loyal leaves! they would resent a funeral sermon preached or dirges sung above them. Their very last word, their death-murmur, is "*Life!*" "We have not been destroyed," they say: "we have been *fulfilled* in fruit that we have made: in it we have eternal life."

They tell the truth. It is *their* fruit. It is the leaves that have made the fruit; and fruit, the culmination of the plant, is the germ of their continued life.

For "fruit" is but *ripened seed,* or the seed-vessels with the parts immediately connected. We call it wheat or barley or chestnut, if the sheath be hard; grapes, blueberries, orange, melon, if the sheath be soft and fleshy. If the outside of the sheath be soft while the inner side is stony, then it is the cherry or the peach. If the coat is a stringy membrane, we have bean-pods. If the calyx, instead of dropping off, hugs the seed-case, and swells out to thick, sweet flesh around it, then we say that our apples and pears and quinces are getting ripe. Or, if a number of the seeds cluster close to-

gèther around a pulpy base, they make our straw-
berries and blackberries. But always, whatever
form or name it takes, fruit is ripened seed;
and the whole summer's labor of the leaves has
been to make that seed.

How have they done it? It is the secret
called "Organization." We touched on it before in speaking of the Resurrections.

If our apples had a tongue between their
red cheeks, they would tell us that once they
were a part of the atmosphere and the ocean;
that they were made of salt sea-vapors and the
long spring-rains and the melting snow-crystals,
— of these, with the carbonic acid and ammo-
nia, which the rain in falling through the air dis-
solved, and a trifle of the soluble minerals lurk-
ing in the earth where the orchard's rootlets
crept. That they *were*,— and now they are our
Baldwins in the cellar, red-cheeked indeed, but
not because they blush to own that lowly origin.
In the process of transmutation from what they
were to what they are, it is the leaves that have
been the chief agent. They have acted like air-
fed mouths for the tree; like skin, to evaporate
its water; perhaps as heart, to help pump up

the sap from down below; but their grand function has been to act as the tree's *stomach* and assimilate its food. When the sap from Mother Earth reaches the tree-top, although slightly changed on the way up through the tree-ducts, it is still little else than crude sap, still in essence mineral; it is not vital; it can make no plant-cells yet. But let this liquid mineral only reach the leaf and have the sunlight fall upon it there, and the wonder happens,— Nature's perpetual miracle of Cana, by which the crude rain-water is " organized " into a subtiler fluid! Somehow, the light-waves do it. The story that the men of science tell of it, their most cunning guess (it is but guess), sounds like a tale of the Arabian Nights. Here it is, made brief : —

The ocean-waves, breaking against the shores of continents, gradually waste those shores away and spread them out into sea-beds, that by and by emerge and make the plains of continents to be. What the ocean-waves, on the grand scale, take the centuries to do, the unseen *heat* and *light-waves* flashing through the ether,—forty, fifty, sixty thousand of them playing in an inch! — five, six, seven hundred billions of them ar-

riving in a second!— these heat and light waves
are supposed to do at every instant to the molecules of the substances on which they strike.
The mimic tides pull down the structure of the
molecules, mingle their atoms together, and
build them over on a different plan. The un-
pilings and repilings go on in perfect harmony,
each element seeking its new mates by fixed
laws of attraction, and mingling with them only
in definite proportions,— as if the old Greek
myth were fact, and some unseen Orpheus sat
by in Nature like him who charmed the rocks by
music into walls. And the more intricate the
"pile," the more complex the molecule's plan,
so much the more "vital" grows the substance.

This, then, is what happens in the leaf. At the
touch of the sun-tides, the earthy sap within it
decomposes and rearranges its constituent atoms
of oxygen and hydrogen, of nitrogen and carbon,
and the rest,— rearranges all in forms more intricate. Thereby, the mineral turns to plant,
the "inorganic" to "organic," the unborn becomes *alive!* And the holy ground where this
drama of perpetual Creation goes on through
all the springs and summers everywhere is —
the Green Leaf. So far as the plant is con-

cerned, to that belongs the credit of the great transfiguration.

The sap, thus vitalized, then descends the tree. According to the chemistry of separate locations, it becomes a hundred different things. Where only three of its four chief elements co-operate, it builds the cell and fibre-walls,—our timber; and makes the sugar and starch and gums and oils to which we owe that part of our food which supports breath and keeps the body warm. But where the fourth element, the nitrogen, is added in, the sap becomes a live substance, "protoplasm," that bathes and lines the cells and coats their nucleus, that enters into the green of leaf and bark, that gathers still more richly in the blossom, and that most of all concentrates in the seed, stocking it with that other part of food, which builds up our flesh and frame. Most of all concentrates in the seed, I say: seed is the *most vital* substance, the very highest being in all the structure of the plant. Its atoms are the outcome of the tree's whole past, the germ of all its future. It is all the old and all the new, in one. For this the rootlets sucked, the sap ran, the twigs budded, the leaves uncurled and veined and spread and filled

the tree, and breathed the sunshine in, and
stood up to greet the showers, and held on
through the tug of storms; and for this the
flowers,—which, as we have seen, are but the
"first families" of leafdom,—for this the flowers arrayed themselves and celebrated the little
weddings, and then chambered their very hearts,
—all for this end, that, at last, the seed-children
might grow and cluster there. All was for
them, and they are the "fruit." In every tree
and violet and grass, in every lichen on its rock,
in every cloudlike pulp that stains the ditches
green, in every weed that swings at anchor in
the seas, this seed-making (or some process kin
to it) has been carried on through all the days
and nights since earliest spring. No man
through all the populations could make one.
Earth and Sun, it takes them both,—it takes a
solar system, all alive, to make a seed!

It is October, and again the deed is done!
The ripened seed-vessels hold the hope of the
world. New root, new stem, new leaf, new
bud, and all the possibilities that sleep in them,
are there wrapped up together. In these, the
next spring's resurrection, next summer's glory,
next autumn's gold and red, lie already in em-

bryo. And everything is safe. Fear not, O
lands! Be not afraid, O fields! Let the leaves
die, and the cold come out of the north!

What sanctity, what wonder past wonder,
hallows the tiny thing so wrought and put together! As we hold a grain of corn or wheat
in our hand, and look at it, and think how it
sums up the year,—

> "Then, suddenly, the awe grows deep,
> Until a folding sense, like prayer,
> Which is, as God is, everywhere,
> Gathers about us; and a voice
> Speaks to us without any noise,
> Being of the silence,"

and, lo! we are at worship,— listening bowed
before a seed!

And should we trace yet farther that little
handful of the year's great harvest which we
shut up in barns and loaves and call "our"
harvest,— and which is as incidental to the trees
and grasses as the birds' nests are that hide in
them,— it would be simply tracing higher this
same process of "*organization.*"

On Thanksgiving Day, as we draw our chairs
around the table, if we stop a moment and
think over the familiar story so wonderful and

praiseful,— think what miracles have been en-
acted to spread the table for us, how last spring
the dinner lay in minerals and was blowing in
the air, and how rains and storms and rise and
set of suns and summer-noons and starry nights
have wrought, till, lo! the squash for our Thanksgiving pies, the cranberries for our sauce,— that
will seem miracle enough! But our turkey, if
we have one, is a greater marvel yet. You know
what the western farmer does, when it costs too
much to transport his corn in bulk? He feeds
it to his swine, and then the crops come on four
legs across the prairies. He is but imitating the
Lord of the Harvest. We cannot go to the grass
and eat it — a herd of Nebuchadnezzars. But
the grass comes to us! God — to give that
Power by which we live a name — God gathers
up the sweetness of a whole hill-side pasture,
of a meadow with all its clovers, of a sea with all
its swaying weeds, and, in the quiet grazers
that go to and from our barn, or the creatures
that cackle out their little lives around it, or
the shy rovers of the woods and waters, offers
us the sweetness economically packed, that is,
more highly organized, built up now into flesh-
atoms,— atoms more complex, more vitalized,

than any that the vegetable world contains. It is but the process of plant-making carried a step farther. Another transfiguration has occurred. To become grass is Heaven to minerals. To become ox is Heaven to the grass. To become man is a kind of unwelcome Heaven to oxen!

For, after dinner, the process of transfiguration will continue. The atoms, once inside of us, will rearrange and organize themselves in structures more and more wonderful, till in man's brain, the most complex of animal structures, we literally have, as one has said, "the condensation of all Space, the grand evolved result of all Time." Listen to what Dr. Clarke says of our human brain: —

"That marvellous and delicate engine, which is only a few inches in diameter, whose weight on an average is only about forty-nine ounces, contains cells and fibres counted by hundreds of millions; cells and fibres that vary in thickness from one one-millionth to one three-hundredth of an inch: it is an engine, every square inch of whose gray matter affords substrata for the evolution of at least eight thousand registered and separate ideas; with substrata in the whole brain for evolving and registering tens of mil-

lions of them, besides the power of recalling
them under appropriate stimulus; an engine
that transmits sensation, emotion, thought, and
volition, by distinct fibres, whose time-working
has been measured to fractions of a second; it
is an engine, a mechanism, that can accomplish
this, and greater wonders still, without conscious
friction, pain, or disturbance, if it be only prop-
erly built and its working be not interfered
with."

From air and rain and rock to human brain,
the series mounts! And, as it is the stored-up
forces of the skies that work the transformation,
Science declares us, in a sense more real than
ever the grand myth fabled, Children of the Sun.

This is "Organization," — the Secret of the
Harvest.

It is the secret of *all* God's harvest-fields; the
way in which he hoards the gains of all his work
from waste. It is the miracle *within* the miracle of Snow and Resurrection and the Flowers.

To much more in ourselves than the structure
of the body it is a clue. Thanks to the Harvest-
Secret, we need not mourn for anything as lost,
— perhaps need mourn for nothing as even
wholly *vanished*.

For instance, our forgotten knowledge. "I have forgotten more than you ever knew," is the poor unction some of us have to quietly lay to our souls to keep up self-respect, when we meet the bright young people all equipped with facts and items. But how is knowledge reckoned best,— in so many school-years, so many books read, so many facts hived up in memory? It *is* good to have facts hived away: theories are worth nothing, unless based on them, and, as a good deal of a man's talk is theorizing, it is helpful to have at hand large quarries of the corner-stones. It is good to remember the books we read, and the faces we have met, and what names go with the faces, and to be able to quote the formulas we learned when young, and to keep the French and German nimble on the tongue. But this is only knowledge, after all, not wisdom,— which is knowledge *become one's self;* it is only learning, not education,— which is learning *transformed to faculty.* It is only the means by which, and not the end for which. It is only leaves, not fruit.

I am not decrying "culture"; but the college-gift is much misvalued. Many a man gets great good from college who at his graduation could hardly enter over again for lack of the statistics and dates and prosody that helped to pass him in; and to whom, in a few years, the Greek and trigonometry become more Greek and unknown quantities than ever,— great good he gets, because, though dropping these, he has meanwhile learned by their aid how to handle his mind. "He knows what he knows, he knows that he doesn't know much, he knows how to get what he doesn't know, and needs." He has learned that snap-judgments are worthless; that nothing is learned until both sides are learned; and he has gained a certain tactile sense by which shams in culture and attainment are detected at quick sight. And this is no bad harvest for the four years spent at college. But, then, just because this is really so large a part of the four years' harvest, many a man who never goes to college gets the essence of the college-education. The very best result of culture is still a *finer common-sense*. "Common-sense,"— the knack of using swiftly, surely, and in conjunction, the common human powers. He who gets that knack may boast with Richter that he has "made the most he could out of the stuff." And what is this common-sense but the concentrated result of a thousand thousand judgments, memories, reflections, the "organized" product and final outcome of all our thinking processes? Such organized and final outcome, as we have seen, is "fruit." In this fruit, a finer common-sense, the books and lessons and days and persons we meet must be harvested, or they are as good as lost,— "nothing but leaves." If so harvested, they have been saved, although in themselves the books, days, persons, fade from memory and drop like leaves entirely off our tree of life.

I said that those who count as the unbred not seldom pass by the highly bred, because life's practical school has proved better than a college to train these common powers. The scholar, for instance, ought to be the one best furnished to see most in Europe,— that great mass of history crystallized in cities and cathedrals and old art and customs. And no doubt the scholar usually does see most. But have you never found your neighbor, the merchant, who began life as a shop-boy, and ever since has lived among his boxes and ledgers, and has made his money, and at sixty sets out with his wife and his five children to go the rounds of Europe, with an English Murray in every pair of hands,— have you never found him coming home with a surprising amount of Europe " organized " in him? He leans back in his chair before the fireplace and tells you he has been to seventy-two cities, and has a picture of each one in his mind, and he knows how many stairs there are in the cathedral-towers, and how high and long St. Peter's is, and where the pictures hang in the galleries : he has " done " Europe. But none the less it is in him now,— culture and joy for the rest of life. And how has he been able to see and bring home so much? Because, while working over those boxes and ledgers and correspondence through the years of business-life, he has harvested the habit of wide-awakeness, the quickness to see minutely, the power to seize firmly and recall vividly details; and he carried abroad with him these sheaves of faculty all barned up in his brain. He hardly knows he has them; at least, he had never suspected they would give him so much of Europe. He is surprised at his friends' surprise that he has seen so much: " Who couldn't? It's there to see," he says. But, none the less, he is conscious of a new feeling of fellowship with those whom he had always before revered afar off as

the happy possessors of that mystic " culture."
The old ledgers are mouldering on the back
shelf in the cellar, the boxes have long since
turned to kindling-wood, while the shoes or can-
dles or drugs they held have gone to their own
place : all have dropped out of the merchant's
life like leaves from the tree, but they have left
the "fruit" of ripened faculty behind them,—
" seed " which has flowered in this late summer
of pleasant knowledge for him.

But our Harvest-Secret is as true of other
parts of life's experience. The trials, the dis-
appointments, the sorrows that make the anni-
versaries sad, the wane of friendships, the temp-
tations that were hardly put under foot, are
leaves which the seasons bring and the seasons
take away. To no purpose? Nay, they give us
the new preciousness of ourselves, our strength
of spiritual fibre, our wiser philosophy of life,
the beautiful lines on the face, the quiet cheer
in the heart, and our increasing helpfulness.

Do you know no woman who has thus been
ripened? Greet her,— she has had small chance
outside of the housekeeping, but you find her
answering you with bright, live, first-brain
thoughts. She can offer you her experience

against your schooling, and is very apt to give
you more than she gets from you. There is so
much of her, because all she has learned by life
is not *in* her merely, but *is herself.* It is a stay-
at-home wife, or a plain-faced, humble-minded
sister; one who thinks herself a mere "chink-
filler." Not for her the out-door exhilaration,
the pleasant changes which the husband or
brother has. But possibly the stamina of the
home lie in her, and not in him. She is, perhaps, the real bulwark, the comfort, the pleasant
crispness of the household life,— and he the limp-
ness of it, although he earn the money. Those
tame home-hours, the lonely drudgeries, that
long patience with the children, the evenings
over their stockings, with the shut book waiting
on the table — while *he* smokes; the mornings
over their lessons — while he reads the paper;
the quiet going around for whims — his, proba-
ably; the word held back on the tongue; — all
this has been slowly vested in strength and self-
control and the sweet shrewdness. She is con-
tinually pulling down her spirit-barns and build-
ing bigger to hold the riches of her harvest.
She is gray-haired before she finds out that
the harvest is a large one. Many generations of
stockings have passed through the basket, the

boys who missed the spelling so are grown up,
and almost all those little doings and bearings
are forgotten: those *leaves* have dropped from
year to year, but the *seed* which they have
made,— her friends are praising that when they
say, "How good she is, how pleasant, and how
we lean on her!" The citizens are praising
that when they elect her boys to the legislature.

My merchant and his wife are only typical.
It is you and I, it is man and woman. In us all,
and all through life, the Secret of the Harvest
is the same. The laws of the seasons reign in
us. "Herein is the Father glorified, that *we*
bear much fruit." The course of life is a thousand trifles, then some crisis,— and again a
thousand trifles and a crisis : nothing but green
leaves under common sun and shadow, and then
a storm or a rare June day. And far more
than the storm or the perfect day the common
sun and common shadow do to make the autumn
rich. It is the "every days" that count. *They*
must be made to tell, or the years have failed.
To *tell:* for that, thought and feeling must become action, and action habit, and habit turn to
principles and character. And if for some of
us, and sometimes for all of us, action cannot

mean *doing*, then remember *bearing*, too, is
action, often its hardest part.

> " I am not eager, bold, or strong,—
>   All that is past !
> I am ready *not* to do,
>   At last,— at last ! "

When that verse comes into the psalm of life,
as, sooner or later, it must come, let us remember that not-to-do *well* is a noble well-doing.
But either by doing or by bearing we must *act*,
in order to harvest anything.   Action is to
thought and feeling what the leaf is to the
crude sap : then of action habit is the blossom,
and of habit character is the fruit.   Character is
the concentrated result of life, its organized de-
posit, its harvest in us, and the seed of after-life.

Between the bearings and the doings, our
years are passing fast.   Death is predetermined
in our frames as in that of the leaves.   From
ten to twenty, we hardly know it.   From twenty
to thirty, we know, but little care.   At thirty,
we begin to care; for already June is well-nigh
past !   Are we leafing yet ?   Are we *only* leafing ?   Or are we so leafing that life's autumn
shall find us rich in pleasant fruit ?   *Are we
ripening Seed ?*